THE DOWNTOWN FAIRY GODMOTHER

"It's only natural to doubt me at first. For one thing, I'm a little old for the job. And then, I'm a little on the plump side. Most fairy godmothers are young and slender and beautiful, with naturally curly hair . . . not like mine."

"Who cares about all that," said Olivia. "You can do magic. Real magic! With a flick of your wand, you can change traffic lights. And you can make a person's fondest wishes come true. . . ."

The fairy godmother smiled, but she had a faraway look. She was thinking of the black cat with the pale green eyes. "Some wishes, yes," she said. "Some wishes, no."

"An outstanding book."
> —The Children's Corner, *Boston Today*

"A delightful fantasy."
> —*Boston Herald-American*

"It is probably advantageous for most of us to realize that the frumpy housewife next door . . . just might be working miracles!"
> —*School Library Journal*

Bantam Skylark Books for Younger Readers
Ask your bookseller for the books you have missed

THE DOWNTOWN FAIRY GODMOTHER

Charlotte Pomerantz
illustrated by Susanna Natti

A Bantam Skylark Book®
Toronto · New York · London · Sydney

*This low priced Bantam Book contains
the complete text of the original hard-cover edition.*
NOT ONE WORD HAS BEEN OMITTED

RL 5, 008-011

THE DOWNTOWN FAIRY GODMOTHER
*A Bantam Book / published by arrangement with
Addison-Wesley Publishing Company, Inc.*

PRINTING HISTORY
Addison-Wesley edition / August 1978
Bantam Skylark edition / February 1983

Published simultaneously in the United States and Canada

*Bantam Books are published by Bantam Books, Inc. Its trade-
mark, consisting of the words "Bantam Books" and the por-
trayal of a rooster, is Registered in U.S. Patent and Trademark
Office and in other countries. Marca Registrada. Bantam
Books, Inc., 666 Fifth Avenue, New York, New York 10103.*

PRINTED IN THE UNITED STATES OF AMERICA

0 9 8 7 6 5 4 3 2 1

A mi hada madrina, Carmen Velázquez

EVERY day on the way to and from school, Olivia stopped to look in the window of the toy shop. There, on the middle shelf, it sat: a stuffed black cat with pale green eyes. The price tag said six dollars and ninety-eight cents. From the moment Olivia saw it, she decided to save every penny of her allowance and buy it.

Today, even though a light spring rain was falling, she stopped at the window on her way home from school. She imagined how it would feel to stroke the soft black fur or cuddle the animal in her arms.

"If only," she said half-aloud, "if only I had a fairy godmother!"

There was a glimmer of blue light, and suddenly there stood before her a plump woman of middle age, dressed all in blue. Blue shoes, blue slacks, blue blouse and blue wings. Bluest of all were her eyes — the color of huckleberries. Everything was blue except the curlers in her hair. They were pink.

In one hand she carried a large pocketbook. In the other, she held a thin walking stick. She hesitated, then took a step forward toward Olivia.

Olivia stared into her huckleberry eyes, but said nothing.

The woman took a step back. "Maybe I'm in the wrong place," she said. "Who did you wish for?"

Olivia held her breath as long as she could. Then she blurted out, "I wished for a fairy godmother!"

The woman smiled. "That's me," she said. "Can't you tell by my wings and my wand?"

Olivia was wide-eyed. "Can you really make wishes come true?"

The woman shifted slightly from one blue shoe to another. "It depends on the wish," she said. "Did you have a particular wish in mind?"

Olivia pointed to the toy shop window. "That black cat with the pale green eyes," she said longingly. "I want it more than anything in the world."

The fairy godmother sighed. A deep, unhappy sigh. Then, reaching into her pocketbook, she pulled out a handkerchief and blew her nose.

"Alas," she said. "I cannot help you."

Olivia had never seen anyone look so unhappy.

"It doesn't really matter," she said, trying to sound cheerful. "I just thought that if you *were* a fairy godmother . . ."

The woman hastily put away her handkerchief and fluffed out her wings.

"I *am* a fairy godmother," she insisted. "But I'm only a beginner and my powers are limited."

"I see," said Olivia. "I didn't know that some fairy godmothers were beginners."

The fairy godmother sighed. "Most people think that once you've read about one fairy godmother, you've read about them all. But it's not that simple."

Her voice changed to that of a kind and patient

teacher. "We come in three grades," she explained. "Grade C is for beginners — like me. Grade B is more experienced. And Grade A" — her voice grew hushed — "they're the ones you read about in fairy tales. Their powers are very great."

Olivia was remembering the fairy tales she had read. "Are they the kind that can turn a prince into a frog?" she asked.

"Yes," said the fairy godmother. "And what's more, a Grade A can turn a frog back into a prince." She thought a moment. "Most of the Grade A's are up in the Bronx, of course."

"The Bronx?" said Olivia. "Why?"

"Because more people live in the Bronx than any other part of New York City. I work downtown, in Lower Manhattan, because there are fewer people."

"I get it," said Olivia. "I'll bet the Grade B's are in Upper Manhattan — between the Bronx and downtown."

"Exactly," said the fairy godmother, delighted that Olivia had caught on.

Olivia was getting very curious. "What sort of things can a Fairy Godmother Grade C — like yourself — do?"

The woman twiddled her wand. "A little of this, a little of that," she said vaguely. "Why don't you try me? Go ahead, wish for something."

Olivia stared at her own reflection in the toy shop window. But all she could think of was the beautiful black cat with the pale green eyes.

"I know," she said suddenly. "My hair. I don't like my hair. It's too straight. I wish . . ." she looked hopefully up at the fairy godmother. "I wish I had curly hair."

The fairy godmother smiled. "That's easy," she said, and reaching into her pocketbook, she pulled out twelve pink curlers.

Olivia groaned softly. "I'm afraid you don't understand," she said. "I wished for *naturally* curly hair."

The fairy godmother shrugged. "Olivia," she said, "if I knew how to change straight hair to *naturally* curly hair, would I be wearing these awful pink curlers?"

"No," said Olivia gloomily. "I guess not."

"Changing straight to curly and curly to straight is strictly Grade A," said the fairy godmother. "But don't give up," she said brightly. "Wish for something else."

Olivia tried to think of a wish. She remembered it was her night to do the dishes. It seemed a small thing to bother a fairy godmother about . . . but it couldn't hurt to ask.

"There *is* something," she said timidly. "It's my night to dry the dishes. Do you suppose you could wave your magic wand and . . ."

But she got no further, because the fairy godmother was shaking her head so vigorously that a pink curler came loose.

"*No housework!*" she declared, tucking the curler back into place.

"No housework," Olivia repeated, for she could think of nothing else to say.

The fairy godmother looked thoughtful. "Maybe it would help if I read you the list of things I *don't* do."

She reached into her pocketbook, took out a piece of paper and read:

ATTENTION ALL CUSTOMERS
My magical powers as a Fairy Godmother Grade C
do not include:
cooking
dishwashing
laundry
ironing
bedmaking
sweeping
dusting
mopping
or any other work of that kind.
In addition, I do not clean fish bowls,
change kitty litter or walk dogs.

She put the paper away, moved closer to Olivia, and spoke in a confiding way. "One of the reasons I took this job was to get out of the house. At first, my husband didn't like the idea at all. He said a woman of my age has no business getting all dolled up in blue and flitting about town.

"But I said, 'Harry,' — that's my husband's name — 'you can't expect me to hang around the house all day waiting for you to come home from work so I can cook dinner. I want to have a life of my own, and there's this great job opening for fairy godmothers.'

"Harry looked at me like I was crazy. 'Fairy godmothers,' he muttered. 'Now I've heard everything.'

"I didn't say anything, but he could see how down-hearted I was, so he came over and put his arms around me. 'Honey,' he said, 'if being a fairy godmother is what you really want to do . . .'

" 'It is, Harry, it is!' I said, hugging him. 'It means getting out of the house, meeting new people, helping them . . .'

" 'Okay, okay,' said Harry."

The fairy godmother patted Olivia's arm. "So you see why I don't do any housekeeping. Harry helps, but I still have a lot of work to do around the house. I don't have time for chores that don't require magic at all."

Olivia nodded, but her thoughts were elsewhere. She was wondering what would be the most polite way to find out what sort of things a Fairy Godmother Grade C *did* do.

Finally she said, "Do you have any — uh — customers?"

"Certainly," said the fairy godmother. "In fact, I have an appointment with one right now. Would you care to come along?"

"Would I!" exclaimed Olivia. "Could I really?"

The fairy godmother nodded and stomped three times on the ground.

"Is that part of the magic?" whispered Olivia.

"Yes," said the fairy godmother. "I always do it when I go from one place to another."

Instantly, as Olivia looked around, she found herself standing on a busy street corner. The fairy godmother shook down her wings, so that they seemed like part of her blouse.

"There," she said, with a final pat. "I'm visible."

"What about me?" asked Olivia. "Can people see me?"

"No," said the fairy godmother. "You're invisible. No one can see you or hear you" — she winked slyly — "except me."

"Are you always visible when you're working?" asked Olivia.

"Yes," said the fairy godmother. "Anyone can see me. My wand, of course, is invisible to everyone, even Mr. Kremsky."

Olivia followed as the fairy godmother walked up to a car double-parked in front of a shoe shop. She pointed to a smallish round man who sat in the driver's seat, his fingers nervously drumming on the steering wheel of the car.

"Hello, Mr. Kremsky," she said. She got in and motioned for Olivia to follow.

Immediately the motor started up, and Mr. Kremsky began to move through heavy traffic.

"Will I have time to see her?" he asked, his voice fairly trembling.

"Yes," said the fairy godmother patiently. "You'll have time."

Olivia was watching the traffic lights. When a light was about to turn red, the fairy godmother waved her wand, and the light stayed green. If the light was already red, she turned it to green. In the same instant the DON'T WALK sign turned to WALK. Olivia couldn't believe it — they had gone for almost a mile, and Mr. Kremsky had not stopped once!

Suddenly a police car pulled up alongside them.

"What's the big hurry, mister," said the policeman, pulling a book of tickets from his pants' pocket. "You've gone nineteen blocks at high speed. Don't you ever stop? Let's see your license."

The fairy godmother leaned across to the driver's window.

"Excuse me, officer," she said, "but you must have seen for yourself that we didn't go through any red lights."

"I saw it all right," said the officer. "And it's mighty fishy. *Mighty* fishy."

The fairy godmother smiled good-naturedly. "It *is* strange. I quite agree." Then she giggled. "Maybe a fairy godmother is fooling with the lights. I know it sounds silly, but there really isn't any other explanation, is there?"

The policeman opened his mouth to say something, but changed his mind. Then, mumbling about "all the crazies let loose in New York City," he walked back to his car.

"Whew," said Mr. Kremsky, using his tie to mop his forehead, "that was close."

He drove one more block and pulled up alongside a bakery. The sign in front said, JENNIE ADAMS — HOMEMADE DESSERTS.

Mr. Kremsky jumped out of the car, slammed the door behind him and dashed into the bakery.

Olivia said nothing, but the fairy godmother could see she was puzzled.

"It's love," she explained. "Mr. Kremsky, who works in a shoe shop, is madly in love with Miss Adams,

who makes homemade desserts. He sees her every day after work and on weekends, too. But that's not enough. He wants to see her during his lunch hour, even if it's only for ten minutes."

"When does he eat lunch?" asked Olivia.

"Miss Adams always gives him a bagful of pastries," said the fairy godmother. "He eats them while he's driving back to work."

"All that driving for only five minutes with Miss Adams," thought Olivia. She wondered what Mr. Kremsky had done before he met the fairy godmother.

It was as if the fairy godmother could read her thoughts, for she said, "It was awful before I came along. Mr. Kremsky would drive to the bakery, just have time to throw her a kiss from the car window and drive right back to the shoe shop. Even so, he was often late for work.

"One day, he just stopped the car in the middle of traffic, threw up his hands and cried out, 'If only, if only I had a fairy godmother!'"

The fairy godmother winked at Olivia. "That," she said, "is when I made my first official appearance."

She adjusted a curler and went on with her story.

"Mr Kremsky poured his heart out. He couldn't bear to give up the lunchtime visits with Miss Adams, but he was terrified of losing his job if he was late again. I thought the problem through and suggested fixing the traffic lights. Mr. Kremsky was overjoyed. He kissed me and danced me around the street until a policeman told him to move along, because he was creating a traffic jam."

The fairy godmother beamed proudly. "Mr. Kremsky says that, ever since he met me, he sells twice as many shoes."

Just then the door of the bakery flew open, and Mr. Kremsky dashed out, his round face covered with lipstick and dollops of whipped cream.

As he drove back to work, not encountering one red light, he popped pastries into his mouth and talked.

"Ah, Jennie," he said. "The loveliest of women. Her eyes are browner than chocolate cupcakes. Her lips are rosier than cherry strudel. And her cheeks — her cheeks are softer than marshmallow pudding." He popped another cream puff into his mouth. "Not to mention her watermelon fruitcake, her pumpkin pie . . ."

The list came to an abrupt end as Mr. Kremsky found a parking space near the shoe shop. Swiftly, they got out of the car, and Mr. Kremsky, waving goodbye, ran back to work.

Olivia's mind was spinning, but all she could think to say was, "Jennie Adams Homemade Desserts — are they really that special?"

The fairy godmother had puffed up her wings and was lifting her foot — but she held it in mid-air. "Harry says my watermelon fruitcake is better," she said. Then the foot came down once, twice, thrice — and Olivia was in front of her apartment house.

"Ooh," she murmured, "I feel like a magical bird in a beautiful blue dream. You really are a fairy godmother after all."

The fairy godmother raised an eyebrow. "You mean you doubted it?" she said sharply.

But before Olivia could explain, her voice had softened. "It's only natural to doubt me at first. For one thing, I'm a little old for the job. And then, I'm a little on the plump side, though Harry likes me the way I am." She smiled coyly. Still, most fairy godmothers are young and slender and beautiful, with naturally curly hair." She reached up and touched a pink curler. "Not like mine."

"Who cares about all that," said Olivia. "You can do magic. Real magic! With a flick of your wand, you can change traffic lights. And you can make a person's fondest wishes come true — like Mr. Kremsky's."

The fairy godmother smiled, but she had a faraway look. She was thinking of the black cat with the pale green eyes. "Some wishes, yes," she said. "Some wishes, no."

Olivia didn't hear her.

"Oh please," she pleaded, "can I go with you tomorrow?"

"If you like," said the fairy godmother. "We'll meet after school in front of the toy shop."

She twiddled her wand. "I have to go now. It's time for dinner. Harry is making fish cakes and spinach pie."

And, with three stomps, she was gone.

THE next day when Olivia arrived at the toy shop, the fairy godmother wasn't there. Within minutes she heard her voice.

"Sorry to keep you waiting," she said, a little out of breath. "But I had to mop the kitchen, start the corned beef for dinner and take Harry's suit and my spare set of wings to the dry cleaners." Her eyes twinkled. "Sometimes I wish I had a fairy godmother to help with the housework."

Then she stomped three times — and they were in front of an old stone building with steep stone steps. The steps led up to a glass-paneled double door.

Behind the door, Olivia could make out an old woman in a wheelchair.

"There she is," said the fairy godmother. "That's dear old Mrs. Chesney."

"Your customer?" asked Olivia.

The fairy godmother nodded. She touched her wand to the lower steps, and — presto — they were changed into a long smooth ramp!

At that moment, the double doors were pushed open, and the old lady, chortling with delight, waved her hand at the fairy godmother and rolled down the ramp onto the sidewalk. She soon disappeared around a corner.

Promptly the ramp became steps again.

"But that's magic!" exclaimed Olivia. "Pure magic!"

The fairy godmother blushed with pleasure.

"It means a lot to Mrs. Chesney," she said. "The poor dear can't get her wheelchair down all those steps, and her landlord, Mr. Hendricks, won't give her the apartment on the street level.

"When I first overheard them, Mrs. Chesney was saying, 'I've been living here ten years, Mr. Hendricks, and I've always kept my place nice and clean and paid the rent on time. Why can't you give me that empty apartment on the street level, so I can wheel myself to the park every day?'

"'Bah,' said Mr. Hendricks. 'You're always complaining. If it isn't one thing, it's two. That's all you old people ever do — complain!' And he just walked away.

"Mrs. Chesney was so angry, she just grabbed the arms of her wheelchair and tried to hold back the tears.

"'If only,' she implored the dark old walls, 'if only I had a fairy godmother!'"

The fairy godmother winked at Olivia. "That," she said, "is when I made my second official appearance."

Her huckleberry eyes sparkled in the sunlight. "It's such a nice day," she said. "Let's sit here till Mrs. Chesney gets back from the park."

"But you're visible," said Olivia. "I mean, everyone can see you."

"It doesn't matter," said the fairy godmother. "I have a right to sit here."

From behind, they heard the heavy tread of a man coming down the steps.

It was Mr. Hendricks. He walked up to the fairy god-mother, pointed an accusing finger and said, "*You* did that, didn't you!"

The fairy godmother blinked up at him. "Did what?" she asked innocently.

"You know very well," said Mr. Hendricks. "You changed my steps into a ramp!"

She patted a curler. "Fiddlesticks," she said. "No-body can change steps into a ramp" — her eyes twinkled naughtily — "unless you believe in fairy godmothers."

"Harumph," he snorted angrily and stomped off down the street.

The fairy godmother found some stray strands of hair and rolled them around a curler. "Old sourpuss," she said.

From down the block came Mrs. Chesney, pushing the arms of her wheelchair and singing. As she got to the steps — bingo — there was a ramp! Up she went, singing lustily:

When the weather is cold
I don't mind being old
Though I don't sing all winter long.

But when warm weather comes
I whistles and hums
And sometimes I breaks into song.

And with a *hey nonny nonny and a nuts to you*! she disappeared inside the doorway.

Once more the ramp became steps. The fairy god-mother stomped three times — and Olivia was standing in front of her apartment house.

"I have to go straight home," said the fairy god-mother. "The corned beef is cooked, but I have to add the cabbage. Harry and I love corned beef and cabbage."

"Can we meet again tomorrow?" asked Olivia.

"That would be nice," said the fairy godmother. "Tomorrow will be a little different. It's my Public Service Day."

And with three stomps, she was gone.

NEXT day, as soon as Olivia arrived at the toy shop, the fairy godmother said, "No time to lose," and stomping three times, Olivia found herself on a subway platform.

"Where are we?" asked Olivia.

"We're at 14th Street and Broadway," said the fairy godmother.

Nearby a girl in pigtails was banging her fist on a candy and chewing-gum machine. Next to her, a man with a briefcase kept pushing and pulling the levers.

"I just lost twenty-five cents!" wailed the girl. "I've been saving all week for a chocolate bar."

The man was now kicking the machine and shouting, "That's the second dime I've lost for a pack of gum!"

A policeman came by. "Okay, everybody," he said, "calm down."

The fairy godmother nudged Olivia. "Aha," she said, "I see my first Public Service of the day." And with a

swift step forward, she reached out with her wand and touched the machine.

"Stand back, lady," said the policeman. "The machine is out of order."

As he spoke, four chocolate bars rolled out, followed by two packs of gum.

"Did you see that?" yelled the girl in pigtails, bending over to scoop up the candy. "Four chocolate bars! It was like a stroke of magic!"

Smiling contentedly, the man with the brief case unwrapped the two packages of gum and, one by one, put all ten pieces into his mouth.

The policeman walked up to the fairy godmother. "Did you tamper with the machine, lady?"

"Why no, officer," she protested. She straightened a curler. "These subway machines are such a bother. As if you men in uniform didn't have enough to do."

The policeman was suspicious. "How come the machine worked the second you pointed at it?"

"How should I know?" she said. "Maybe a fairy godmother just touched her wand to it — and *poof*!"

The policeman fiddled with his night stick and, shaking his head, walked away.

The fairy godmother and Olivia walked on, stopping in front of a row of five phone booths.

All five were out of order. The receiver had been torn off one phone; it lay on the shelf, a long piece of cord dangling from it.

One woman was frantic. "We're having a dinner party tonight, and if I don't call my husband and tell him to put the roast in the oven, we'll have mustard and pickles for dinner!"

"You think you've got problems," said a young man. "I told my girl friend we'd go out for pizza, and now my boss tells me I have to work overtime. I can't even reach her to tell her."

A large red-faced man was pacing up and down. "My crazy daughter," he moaned. "If I don't call her up every day at this time, she forgets to walk the dog and he pees all over the carpet."

A telephone repairman came along.

"I'll try to get one or two of these working," said the repairman. "But that one with the receiver ripped off — forget it."

The fairy godmother stepped forward and tapped lightly on each booth.

Then she picked up the disconnected receiver and handed it to the lady who was having a dinner party. "Just speak into this, Madam," she said. "It works like a charm."

From inside a booth, the repairman was yelling, "I didn't do a thing, and it works!" He ran from one telephone to another. "So does this one, and this one . . ."

The flustered woman was outside the booth shouting, "You're not going to believe this, dear, but I'm talking to you from a disconnected telephone receiver! You hear me . . . it's the craziest thing I've ever seen. Now about that roast . . ."

Above all the other noises, there was a heartrending groan. "Oh, no! You mean he already peed! My new shag carpet . . ."

The fairy godmother and Olivia headed for the exit. But the long steep escalator which took people to the street level wasn't moving.

A policewoman was trying to reassure the crowds.

"An engineer is on the way," she shouted. "Please stand back. Everybody stand back."

The fairy godmother took Olivia's hand, pushed through the mass of people and stepped onto the escalator.

"Get off that step!" snapped the policewoman. "Can't you see the escalator is not moving?"

"Oh, but it is," said the fairy godmother, as she and Olivia were carried swiftly upwards.

A confused but delighted crowd followed them.

When they reached the top, Olivia and the fairy godmother made their way to the street.

The fairy godmother breathed in the fresh air and yawned. "This day of Public Service always leaves me exhausted," she said. "Ready?"

Olivia nodded — and there she was, in front of her apartment house.

Her eyes were shining with wonderment. "Oh, fairy godmother," she said, "there are so many things you can do, and so many people you can help."

The fairy godmother smiled wearily. "That's true," she said. "But there are so many more things I can't do."

She was thoughtful. "Pot holes, for example. I have no power to fix pot holes. I see people tripping on them, sometimes falling down, and there's nothing I can do. It's the same with broken toys, stomachaches, crying babies, lost pennies, and so much more . . ."

She looked at Olivia with the saddest of smiles. "It's also true of the beautiful black cat with the pale green eyes."

Olivia blushed. "I've always been so busy wishing my own wishes that I never realized how wonderful it could be to see other people's wishes come true."

The fairy godmother's face changed from sadness to the keenest of joy. "Now you know why I took this job," she said.

And with a warm smile and three stomps, she was gone.

WHEN Olivia awoke the next morning, she couldn't believe what she saw. On the pillow next to her was the stuffed black cat — only its eyes were no longer pale green. They were the color of huckleberries! When she reached over to touch it, a letter fell out from under her

pillow. With a curious bittersweet feeling, Olivia sat up and read it.

Dear Olivia,

You'll never guess what!

I got promoted from a Fairy Godmother Grade C to a Fairy Godmother Grade B. That means I won't be working downtown anymore. (Don't worry — someone else will take care of my customers.) They've moved me uptown, and I get to do a lot more magic. For example, I can cancel piano lessons and change a tricycle into a ten-speed bike!

I asked my boss if I could perform one bit of Grade B magic while I was still Grade C. At first she said no. But I told her it was for a *very* special person, and finally she agreed.

Which explains, dear Olivia, the beautiful black cat which you've wanted for so long. (I don't know how the pale green eyes got changed to huckleberry — maybe I held my wand a little crooked.)

Olivia patted the cat and continued reading.

If I do well uptown, they'll promote me to the Bronx, which is as high as a fairy

godmother can go and still be in New York City. If I ever do get to the Bronx, I'll be a Fairy Godmother Grade A, which means I'll be able to do most anything, such as changing a prince into a frog. (I wonder how many princes live in the Bronx.)

I'll still wear my all-blue outfit, but no curlers. The boss says they take away from my image.

Well, bye now, and wish me luck.

Your devoted
Fairy Godmother (Grade B)

P.S. Harry is funny. He wouldn't come out and say he was happy I got the promotion. He just brought me a bottle of champagne and a dozen blue roses.

Olivia picked up the black cat and hugged it to her. "Thanks, and good luck uptown, Fairy Godmother," she said.

Charlotte Pomerantz was born in New York and attended *L'Institut des Sciences Politiques* before graduating from Sarah Lawrence. She has since edited and authored a variety of books for adults and children. THE PRINCESS AND THE ADMIRAL was the winner of the 1975 Jane Addams Award, and THE DAY THEY PARACHUTED CATS ON BORNEO was selected as an Outstanding Book of the Year by the *New York Times*. Ms. Pomerantz and her husband, Carl Marzani, live in New York City with their two young children, Gabrielle and Daniel.

Susanna Natti lives in Cambridge, Massachusetts. She studied illustration at the Rhode Island School of Design. The illustrations for her first book for children, THE DOWNTOWN FAIRY GODMOTHER, are done in pen and ink, the method she uses most frequently.

WANT TO READ THE MOST EXCITING BOOKS AROUND? CHOOSE CHOOSE YOUR OWN ADVENTURE®

Everybody loves CHOOSE YOUR OWN ADVENTURE® books because the stories are about you. Each book is loaded with choices that only you can make. Instead of reading from the first page to the last page, you read until you come to your first choice. Then, depending on your decision, you turn to a new page to see what happens next. And you can keep reading and rereading CHOOSE YOUR OWN ADVENTURE® books because every choice leads to a new adventure and there are lots of different ways for the story to end.

Buy these great CHOOSE YOUR OWN ADVENTURE® books, available wherever Bantam Skylark books are sold or use the handy coupon below for ordering:

Bantam Skylark Paperbacks
The Kid-Pleasers

Especially designed for easy reading with large type, wide margins and captivating illustrations, Skylarks are "kid-pleasing" paperbacks featuring the authors, subjects and characters children love.

☐ 15168	HUGH PINE Janwillen Van de Wetering	$1.95
☐ 15188	DON'T BE MAD IVY Christine McDonnell	$1.95
☐ 15172	INCREDIBLE JOURNEY Sheila Burnford	$2.25
☐ 15097	CHARLIE AND THE CHOCOLATE FACTORY Roald Dahl	$2.25
☐ 15174	CHARLIE AND THE GREAT GLASS ELEVATOR Roald Dahl	$2.25
☐ 15165	JAMES AND THE GIANT PEACH Roald Dahl	$2.75
☐ 15182	ENCYCLOPEDIA BROWN BOY DETECTIVE Donald Sobol	$1.95
☐ 15176	ENCYCLOPEDIA BROWN CASE OF THE SECRET PITCH Donald Sobol	$1.95
☐ 15060	ABEL'S ISLAND William Steig	$1.95
☐ 15194	BIG RED Jim Kjelgaard	$2.50
☐ 15067	DRAGON, DRAGON AND OTHER TALES John Gardner	$1.75
☐ 15206	IRISH RED: SON OF BIG RED Jim Kjelgaard	$2.25
☐ 01803	JACOB TWO-TWO MEETS THE HOODED FANG Mordecai Richler	$2.95
☐ 15050	THE EYES OF THE AMARYLLIS Natalie Babbitt	$1.75
☐ 15065	TUCK EVERLASTING Natalie Babbitt	$1.95
☐ 15096	DON'T STAND IN THE SOUP Bob Stine	$1.75
☐ 15167	THE TWITS Roald Dahl	$1.95
☐ 15159	BANANA TWIST Florence Parry Heide	$1.95
☐ 15179	THE HOUSE WITHOUT A CHRISTMAS TREE Gail Rock	$1.95
☐ 15078	THE LITTLE RASCALS Romeo Muller	$2.50

Bantam—SK-2/83